Rocket's 100th Day of School

To Lee, Elinor, and Charlie . . . my 1, 2, 3
(in no particular order)

Copyright © 2014 by Tad Hills

Visit us on the Web!
randomhousekids.com
Educators and librarians, for a variety of teaching tools, visit us at RHTeachersLibrarians.com

Library of Congress Cataloging-in-Publication Data
Hills, Tad, author, illustrator.
Rocket's 100th day of school / Tad Hills. — First edition.
pages cm
Summary: Rocket the dog is excited about the 100th day of school and enlists the help of his friends to collect one hundred special things to bring to class, from heart-shaped stones found with Mr. Barker to feathers Owl provides, but will he find enough items in time?
ISBN 978-0-385-39095-8 (hc) — ISBN 978-0-385-39096-5 (glb) — ISBN 978-0-385-39097-2 (pbk.)
ISBN 978-0-385-39098-9 (ebk)
[1. Collectors and collecting—Fiction. 2. Hundredth day of school—Fiction. 3. Schools—Fiction. 4. Friendship—Fiction. 5. Dogs—Fiction.] I. Title. II. Title: Rocket's one hundredth day of school.
PZ7.H563737Rof 2014
[E]—dc23
2014010940

The text of this book is set in Century.
The illustrations in this book were rendered in colored pencils and acrylic paint.

MANUFACTURED IN CHINA
10 9 8 7 6 5 4 3 2 1
First Edition

Rocket's 100th Day of School

Tad Hills

schwartz & wade books · new york

Rocket needs to find
100 special things
for the 100th day
of school.

He finds

the perfect spot to keep

his special things.

Or maybe not.

"You can keep your
things here," says Bella.

Rocket finds pencils.

He finds a book.

He finds acorns.

He puts them
in the tree.

Emma helps Rocket
find red leaves
and pinecones.

Mr. Barker helps Rocket
find heart-shaped stones.

Fred helps Rocket
find sticks that look
like numbers.

Rocket writes down
all 26 letters
of the alphabet.

He puts everything
in the tree.

Some days

he writes down words

he likes.

Owl gives

Rocket feathers.

They all go

in the tree.

Finally,
the 100th day of school
is here.

Rocket runs to the tree.

He counts everything

he put in there.

10 pencils
1 book
18 red leaves
5 pinecones
3 stones
5 sticks
26 letters
23 words
+4 feathers
_____
95 things

"Where are the acorns?"

Rocket asks.

"Have you seen the
acorns, Bella?"

"The what?"
Bella asks.

"The acorns," says Rocket.

"Acorns?" asks Bella.

"Yes," says Rocket.

"YES!
    I ATE THEM!"
shouts Bella.

"I LOVE ACORNS
SO MUCH!"

"I need those acorns!"
says Rocket.

"It is the 100th day
of school.
Now I only have
95 things!"

Rocket has an idea.

"Follow me, everyone,"
says Rocket.

"We are all

going to school."

"95 plus four <u>old</u> friends makes 99," counts Rocket.

"And one <u>new</u> friend
makes 100!"